They Fell like Stars From the Sky

& Other Stories

Sheikha Helawy

Translated from Arabic by Nancy Roberts
Illustrated by Anna Morrison

NEEM TREE
PRESS

Published by Neem Tree Press Limited, 2023

Copyright Original Arabic Text © Sheikha Helawy
Copyright English Translation © Nancy Roberts
Copyright Illustrations © Neem Tree Press

3 5 7 9 10 8 6 4 2

Neem Tree Press Limited
95A Ridgmount Gardens, London, WC1E 7AZ
United Kingdom
info@neemtreepress.com
www.neemtreepress.com

A catalogue record for this book is available from the British Library.

ISBN 978-1-915584-01-4 Paperback
ISBN 978-1-915584-02-1 Ebook
ISBN 978-1-911107-62-0 US Ebook

Printed and bound in Great Britain.

They Fell like Stars From the Sky

& Other Stories

Translator's Preface

Originally published in Arabic in 2015, *They Fell Like Stars From the Sky and Other Stories* is the first of Sheikha Helawy's four short story collections. With its no-nonsense, gripping, yet poetic style, it ushers us starkly into the world of the Bedouin village where Helawy grew up and the experiences of girls and women in that context.

Very few authors have written about the experiences of women in Palestinian Bedouin society. Helawy, by contrast, consciously zeroes in on the experience of Palestinian Bedouin women in the present day. As one critic observes, Helawy "may be the only female writer who has delved this deeply with her pen into the worlds of Bedouinness in our local Palestinian literature."[1] The power of *They Fell Like Stars From the Sky* may derive in part from the autobiographical nature of many of its stories, which Helawy penned as a process of reconciliation with her own Bedouin identity and past.

More specifically, the Bedouinness Helawy depicts is that of the forgotten village of Dhail El E'rj from which she, and all

---

1   Kawthar Jabir Qashshum, "Writer Sheikha Helawy: Queen of the Darkness and Our Radiant Face", Al-Ittihad. Last modified December 27, 2019. https://short.link.alittihad44.com/FLS1

its other residents, were forcibly displaced by the Israeli occupation in the 1990s in preparation for its demolition and erasure to make room for an Israeli railway. Even before its demolition and erasure, the village had been given the apartheid-like designation of "unrecognized," and then deprived of electricity, water, and all other services, while the nearby (illegal) Israeli settlement was fully serviced and developed.

Helawy has received letters from women and girls all over the Arab world who tell her she is speaking on their behalf and urge her to keep writing. Indeed, Helawy's name has become uniquely associated with the feminist voice of rebellion against repression and tribalism. She recognizes that she may not be reaching the women about whom she writes, since illiteracy would prevent them from reading her work. However, she sees herself as owing them a great debt. When receiving the Almultaqa Short Story Award in 2019 for her short story collection, *Order C345*,[2] she dedicated the prize to her Bedouin village, and especially to her family, "whose illiteracy taught me to revere the word...."[3]

Another special contribution of *They Fell Like Stars From the Sky* is its intentional use of the local Bedouin dialect in some of the dialogue. Being aware of this intentionality on the author's part, I chose to reproduce certain colloquial phrases in transliterated form from time to time in hopes of conveying to readers some of the earthy immediacy of the narrative. How well I've succeeded in achieving this aim, I'm not certain. However, I felt particularly motivated to try given

---

2   M Lynx Qualey, "Palestinian Sheikha Hussein Helawy Wins Almultaqa Prize for 'Order C345'", ArabLit Quarterly, no. 4 (2019).

3   Jabir, "Writer Sheikha Helawy: Queen of the Darkness."

the warm nostalgia that's evoked in me when I encounter this type of rural dialect, which reminds me of conversations with my beloved Palestinian mother-in-law and others from my extended Arab family.

I hope this book will be received in the spirit of resistance and determined love that inspired its writing and translation.

Nancy Roberts

Contents

To the contrary little girl I left behind under the oak tree in the village of Dhail El E'rj.
The village died, and so did the tree, but she remained, waiting for the light beneath the wings of "the queens of darkness."

I didn't read great books in my childhood.
There were no great books to be read in shacks that pleaded
just to survive from one flood to the next.
I sneaked more than once into the modest library my
uncle kept in a little house in a village that would soon
be swallowed up by the earth, never to return. And into a
bookmobile that my mother insists to this day never existed.
There were no great books in my childhood. But there were
women as great as books.

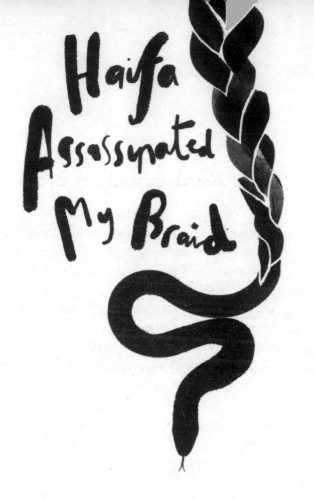

One

Haifa Assassinated My Braid

∽

M y mother and I crossed the street between the bus stop and the district's only barber shop. Each of us had taken refuge in a silence that shielded us from the misery of discussing the matter further. Ever since I'd transferred to the Sisters of Nazareth School in Haifa, I'd been pressing her about it. I'd ask, and she'd refuse. I'd beg, and she'd curse. I'd cry, and she'd fall silent.

Recently divorced, she'd used up her share of transgressions, and she didn't know how she was going to cope with another one. What excuse could she muster for a girl who'd been led astray by Haifa? She wasn't convinced, but she'd agreed to it. She'd taken a liking to the taste of rebellion. Or at least, she'd come to hate the taste of subservience.

The way to the barber shop was a familiar one, but on this particular morning, it felt different.

I twirled around in the swivel chair to see my braid lying on the floor like the serpent in Paradise, tempting someone to touch it or crush it. My hand went to feel the place where the amputation had occurred, and it drew back as if it had been stung. I felt a rush of terror that nearly knocked me out of the

1

chair. I glimpsed the reflection of my mother's face in the huge mirror as she stifled a gasp, her palm over her mouth.

"Here's your little braid," the barber said with a touch of admiration and enthusiasm. It plummeted to the floor, the scissors in his hands taking pride in another masculine victory. Steeped as he was in the Bedouin mentality that equates braids with virginity, he sensed the grievousness of the calamity that had just occurred. Even so, he'd scored an advantage that few barbers in the area enjoyed. The braid he had captured would, for long years thereafter, frame the picture of a pretty girl with short hair that hung above his big mirror.

I burst into silent sobs as my mother looked daggers at me from behind as if to say, "All right, all right, just wait till we're out of here…!"

Only this time, my mother's threat didn't scare me, since she was my partner in crime. She'd even chosen the barber, the day, and the hour. Her consent had been forced. Even so, it was a consent that would shield me from certain punishment. My amputated braid had taken a piece of my soul with it. I ached in silence, not daring to look in the mirror in front of me. My mother's grieved rage challenged me from one direction, while my bereaved head challenged my childish impulsiveness from another.

Haifa, treacherous friend, had lured me in, then suddenly announced her repentance.

Hoping to console myself over my loss, I tried to muster the defiance that had brought me to where I now sat. I thought about how jealous I'd been of girls with a look that was different from mine. Yet even the pictures of pretty girls with short bobs that had captivated me for so long whenever I passed the barber shop, luring me away from my Bedouin ways, couldn't justify my sin.

After that day I avoided walking past his shop to keep from getting upset all over again.

Haifa, Haifa, how could you have abandoned me now?

What solace was there for me in a slaughtered braid?

"*Allah yaksif `umritch ya-al-ba`ida*—May God cut your life short!" my mother would say in her Bedouin dialect. She started pounding me with those words a thousand times a day. God never answered her prayer, but she never tired of repeating it!

Chattering on, the barber said, "I mean, a young lady like you, what does she need with a braid like that?"

Every morning I used to come sit on the threshold that separated the bedroom/sitting room from the kitchen/bathroom, and my mother would stand over me. The resulting elevation enabled her to get better control over the nappy hair that came down to the small of my back. It was so thick she could just barely gather it in her fist. As she got hold of one strand, another would escape her grip. When she'd finally gotten hold of it all, she'd run her comb through it. With every journey of the comb, I would reel in pain. But with every "ouch" that escaped from me, her grip would tighten, the comb would press harder, and I'd be quiet again. She wouldn't release me until she'd "put my hair away" in a braid fit for a well-mannered girl.

"What? Your daughter wants to do like the city girls?" one of my uncles asked my mother, warning her against trials to come.

The students at Haifa's Sisters of Nazareth School were a mix of city kids and country kids who commuted every morning from neighboring villages, all of them having their own dreams and their own reasons for being there. When I arrived at the school entrance, the doors to heaven and hell would

3

open together. Temporarily erasing from my memory a shack that was home to me, my brother, and my mother, I would disavow the Bedouin identity that had been bequeathed to me from all eternity and, with it, my disgraceful Bedouin dialect.

The only things that blew my cover were my name and my braid. I felt as though my spirit were receiving a lashing with the muffled laughter and the mocking question, "Sheikha … ha haha! What are you—an old lady?!"

It did no good to tell my classmates I was descended from a line of desert monarchs, and that my name was a badge of honor.

As for my braid, it was a Bedouin legacy that had been breaking my back. My hand fiddled nervously with short hair that brushed against my neck, its loose strands flirting with the features of a face that looked too harsh to belong to a young girl.

"So, are you satisfied now? Are you like the Haifa girls? Is that what you wanted, *Allah yaksif ʿumritch?*!"

So, I'd become like the Haifa girls. Or nearly so.

At least, that's what I believed, or nearly so. But my hand still went looking for my braid, only to draw back as if it had been stung.

I'u Be There

Two

I'll Be There

ىء

I didn't feel guilty about lying to her, and to her in particular. We all hid some things from our mothers. And even
the things we chose to tell them about, we would wrap with
feigned care—the way we wrap a cheap gift—in some snow-
white lies.

Whenever I hid something from her, I saw it as falling
under the category of "white lies," that didn't merit the punishment that would descend on me if the untruth had caused
her some painful embarrassment. I needed lies just the way
I needed to be one of them: Tony, Julia, Maha, Ihab, Nadira,
Charlie. I needed them in order to slip out of my Bedouin tent
and live my temporary exile in peace. I needed them in order
to kill the tribes and still be loved by her. Yet her love was as
cold and hurtful as it was deep. No sooner had it bestowed a
hesitant smile or kiss then it would turn to nothing, just the
way I turned to nothing when she called down curses on me in
her moments of rage.

"You made me look bad in front of the Sister! What's she
going to say about me now? That I don't know how to raise my
daughter?"

"*Yumma*—Mama…"

"*Humma wa hayya jadra!*"[1] she shot back angrily. "Aren't you ashamed of yourself? Do you want to turn into a tramp…? Do you lie to me? *Wallahi laksif `umritch*—I swear to God, I'm going to kill you!"

The British nun Sister Bern and my mother were ages apart in terms of cultural awakening, but they saw eye to eye on the need to educate and refine me. Whenever I broke the school's strict rules, Sister Bern would call me a gypsy, which was what my mother was afraid I'd turn into some day. I was escaping the Bedouins' snare only to fall into the clutches of those free-spirited Romanis.

My colorful earrings and bracelets multiplied with every passing month, while the Sister who had vowed herself to Christ and the convent would take them off me one by one with a painful cruelty meant to purge me of the filth of "the backward East." Then—a statue of the Madonna and baby Jesus to her right, and a crucifix to her left—she would toss them into a box that served as a repository for minor offenses. My hair kept getting crazier and wilder, my mother more and more terrified, and her oaths more and more solemn: "I swear to God, I swear to God, I'd rather die than be seen walking down the street with you when your hair looks like that!"

In order to get past the hang-ups and suspicions of these two women—one, a European woman who was a messenger of Christ, and the other, a Bedouin woman who was a messenger

---

1   Literally, "a fever and a black snake!" In other words, "I hope you're smitten with a fever and bitten by a black snake!"

of fear—lying became a vital necessity. To get past myself and my fear, I had to lie.

As fate would have it, one chilly Sunday morning my mother met with the nun at the school, who explained to her in her British English that there were no teachers or students at the school that day. Despite the language barrier, my mother understood that her daughter, who had left home that morning on the pretext that the teachers were giving review sessions for the upcoming high school exams, had been lying to her. As my mother saw things at that moment, lying was the same as doing something shameful. There was no difference between them: Lying prepares the way for shameful acts, while shameful acts are exposed along with the lies.

To the nun, this sin of mine provided the perfect excuse to be sterner and crueler than ever in her treatment of me. She seemed to derive some sort of holy pleasure from reprimanding me in her office the next day.

"Look at yourself!" she said. "You're like a gypsy!"

Each of these two women imagined me to be committing a particular sin depending on her own view of the world: My mother pictured me loitering with girlfriends who bore the stigma of being too citified and out of control, while the Sister figured I was having secret trysts with a boyfriend who was toying with my virgin feelings.

We crossed Abbas Street on our way to the bus station. My mother's steps were distant, and so was the expression on her face. I wasn't afraid of her punishment, which I'd experienced so many times I knew it by heart. She walked at a brisk pace, looking behind her every now and then. Whenever I started to close the distance between us, she would broaden her strides. As I trailed her, I began singing a song Nadira and I had listened to more than ten times that day. The radio at our house, which was monopolized by my mother, gave me no chance to hear the songs coming out of the crazy West:

> *Time, it needs time*
> *To win back your love again*
> *I'll be there, I'll be there*
> *Love, only love*
> *Can bring back your love someday*
> *I'll be there, I'll be there.*

When we reached the station, she turned and whispered angrily, "And you're singing too! *Walitch*, haven't you got any shame? Is that what you've been learning from those trashy friends of yours?"

Would she have believed me if I'd told her I learned it from the one friend who was farthest from sin and closest to God? She wouldn't believe it until years later, when there was no longer a need to lie.

They Fell
like Stars
From the Sky

Three

They Fell Like Stars From the Sky

A thin stream of viscous blood trickled over the ground, then quickly dried, leaving a red spot in the dirt. Another spot was still visible on Jawahir's dress: big and round, low on her abdomen. Her mother uttered a silent prayer that the unthinkable hadn't happened.

The women exchanged catty winks that no one but they could decipher; the girls hid behind the bashfulness of virginity; the boys stole quietly away from a situation that only women could address.

As for Habbaba Hisn,[2] she just shook her head. Who but she could have known what evil lay concealed within a cursed primitive swing? Thanks to the wisdom she had gleaned over the years by virtue of her age and the hours she'd spent sitting with the men of the village, Habbaba Hisn could see what others couldn't.

Some boys, who spent the better part of their day looking for amusement in the trash discarded by the Israeli settlement that overlooked them from a nearby hilltop, had rigged up a

---

2   Habbaba—a title used to refer to a maternal great-grandmother.

swing using a gigantic truck tire. They'd pulled it out of a scrap heap that marked the border between the village and the civilized world. Then they'd hung it with thick ropes from the huge oak tree.

Five or six of them would sit on the swing while two of them pushed it.

The sky seemed close, closer than the ground. Their feet, which had been accustomed to sneaking across borders, now touched the canvas of the sky. The swing took them soaring up and up until the Jewish settlement was beneath their feet. The screams of rapturous delight brought to mind the legend of the jinni that was said to live inside the old oak tree.

"The tree is haunted."

This is what adults would tell children to scare them away from their private sessions under the tree's shade. Even so, the tree continued to be a major attraction.

Jawahir and her girlfriends stood watching the boys as they went soaring into the village sky.

"Have you ever ridden on a swing?" one of them whispered.

"No, never. But I wish I could!"

"I'm scared…and if we fell…"

"We'd fall from the sky, like stars."

"Yeah…."

Whenever the swing rose high, their eyes would measure the distance it covered between one end of the sky and the other, their hands clutching tightly to the hems of their dresses.

"And what if the wind blew my dress up?!" one of them wondered aloud in horror.

The screams of delight that filled the village had awakened a suppressed waywardness in the girls, and every journey the swing made from one end of the sky to the other brought them closer to the tree of sin.

True to her stubborn nature, Jawahir stood there mulishly, determined not to leave until she'd gotten a taste of the air above the tree. She knew instinctively that the swing bordered on the shameful. But no way was that going to stop her. Hadn't she had the guts to dance in front of strangers at her aunt's wedding? Of course, the men of the family had held an emergency gathering that same evening and decided to contain the affair by sending her home straight away.

At midday the boys dispersed among the near and distant pastures with provisions for the shepherds.

As the swing danced its devilish gig, the girls crowded onto it. After all, tomorrow might never come, and the Devil wasn't going to stick around. The swing moved gracefully between the two ends of the sky, the balmy April noon breeze billowing their skirts and tickling the fuzz on their thighs. The sky had never been so clear.

Was it April? Was it the village sky? Or might the swing have gone beyond it to some other sky?

"See?" Jawahir whispered into her girlfriend's ear. "I told you this tree was haunted!"

A shudder went through their bodies. Might the jinn really be this nice?

But before the swing had completed its circuit, the rope snapped, scattering the girls around the tree's perimeter. The giant tire landed in the wadi, leaving the rope dangling from the tree in a dance of the jinn.

The women came running to make sure their daughters hadn't been hurt. At the same time, they were so furious that they received them with a slap here and a curse there. By this

15

time, the only girl still on the ground was Jawahir. She'd fallen quite some distance from the tree, where some gnarled boulders had been lying in wait for her. She got up with difficulty, only to find to her alarm that some rocks were stained with her blood.

She examined her hands and feet but didn't find a scratch. Then, without thinking, she ran her hand over her lower abdomen, and it came back spattered with blood. She felt no pain, but the gasp released by the women around her went straight through her, like a knife slaughtering her childhood.

Although her blood was there, she was gone, buried in shame and humiliation.

God help her mother!

When she saw what had happened, she screeched, "You made my blood run dry! *Allah ynashshif dammitch*! May God do the same to you!" And she meant it like she'd never meant it before.

If only her blood *had* run dry. If only it had dried up and turned to stone. That would have been better than it spilling this way.

Back in their hut, her mother examined her in the presence of Habbaba Hisn. The wound was on her thigh. There was a collective sigh of relief. It was deep, so Habbaba Hisn covered it liberally with coffee grounds, then pressed on it until the bleeding stopped.

"God protected her, and us too," her mother murmured.

Making a point to be heard by the other women, Habbaba said, "Thank God, the girl's all right."

A few days later, the swing went back into operation and was again touching the sky. At noon, the boys scattered among the nearby pastures with provisions for the shepherds. Then

16

the women crowded onto the swing, laughing and joking with the jinni of the tree. Jawahir and her girlfriends stood watching from afar, their eyes measuring the distance between the two ends of the sky and their hands clutching all the more tightly to the hems of their dresses.

Likewise observing the women from afar, Habbaba Hisn shook her head and muttered to her prayer beads, "God protect them."

Four

Pink Dress

⁓

It was a plain, straight-up-and-down pink dress that came down to the knees. Nothing complicated about it. Two oblique lines ran from the shoulders to the knee. It had an oval-shaped neckline and sleeves that extended out by a couple of inches. It was an ordinary, boring pink dress. What made it out of the ordinary was the fact that Thurayya would be wearing it to her maternal uncle's wedding. She hadn't paid much attention to its details. It was pink, and that was all that had mattered to her. So as she tried it on in the store, she hadn't bothered to look down at her legs. The shop had been so packed with customers, there hadn't been time, or room, to stop and ponder every dress. Each of them had made her choice quickly, tried it on even more quickly, and then gone to squat in a corner while she compared her own dress's charms with that of a cousin or an aunt.

Back at home in front of the dingy mirror, she was shocked by the glaring mismatch between her swelling bosom and the unsightly fuzz that covered her legs. It ruined her lady-like appearance, and people were bound to raise their eyebrows and exchange mischievous glances.

19

Her mother insisted she was still too young for the pain and hassle that went with making oneself beautiful. Besides, the temptations beauty brings with it might break her child-like spirit, and it frightened her to think about them.

"It's too early," Thurayya's mother announced. She intended to be heard by her daughter's paternal aunt, who was in charge of preparing and applying the sugar paste. She would spread it on youthful bodies, then pull it off with a deft snap of the wrist that had won her an unequalled reputation among the women of the village.

"It's too early" would be enough to prevent anyone from trying to persuade the aunt of her sacred obligation to ensure her young niece's ladylike appearance.

Thurayya wondered how she could have agreed to buy that dress, or any other dress that would have landed her in this sort of predicament. How was she going to resolve the contradiction between a full-blown womanhood on top and a flawed one down below? Thirteen was old enough to have to put up with the misery of monthly menstrual cycles, suffocating brassieres, and the first flutters of the heart. But it wasn't old enough to have smooth, shiny legs. At least, not in her mother's book.

With the exception of the heart flutters, womanhood seemed to be perpetually postponed.

There was no time to buy a replacement, and she wasn't about to go to the wedding with grungy-looking legs, even if—as her younger maternal aunt assured her—the night promised to conceal her flaws.

A solution began running through Thurayya's mind and amid the little hairs climbing up her legs. She dismissed it at first, but it kept coming back and asserting itself all the more forcefully. Her only hope lay in her father's old razor, which had been getting progressively rustier around the edges since he exited their lives. She didn't know why her mother still held onto it. Her ten-year-old brother hadn't sprouted a single whisker yet, so apart from a maturity yet to be, the rusty razor was evidence of manhood's absence rather than its presence.

When she was sure her mother and brother were out, Thurayya plopped down in front of an open door, where the daylight could expose anything that protruded from the skin on her legs. She grasped the razor blade with trembling hands, not sure how to begin: was she supposed to shave from top to bottom, or the other way around? Full of trepidation, she began passing the blade over her right leg. She pictured the harvester in the wheat field opposite the village swallowing up ears of grain and leaving a smooth rectangular strip between two walls of uncut stalks. The thought gave her the giggles. The clean-cut rows running down her legs gradually grew closer together until they merged into an expanse of smooth harvested ground. She was captivated by the wonder of it all. To think of all the beauty that had been concealed by ugly little hairs whose ugliness she'd never even noticed until after they were gone! How could she bear to have them grow back and ruin her nice shiny legs? She couldn't imagine letting such a lovely sight be marred all over again.

It hadn't been a difficult task. Within minutes she'd achieved the perfection of womanhood. Eyes would widen in astonishment and admiration at her beautifully symmetrical, perfectly refined appearance. She liked the feeling of being a complete woman.

Her mother's silence suggested that she approved of the result even if it had been achieved through an act of rebellion, and that she'd reconsidered her earlier rejection of her daughter's request. She didn't ask who had done it, or how. She just cast a quick glance at the girl's legs, then looked off into the distance the way she usually did when she wanted to avoid some inconvenient reality.

As for Thurayya, she didn't pay much attention to the details of the wedding. She was too preoccupied with her own new details.

After the wedding, she collapsed exhausted onto the mattress in her grandmother's house, running her hands over her legs with relish. Then suddenly her hand paused at a raised patch below the back of her knee. It protruded like a missed row of corn stalks in an otherwise perfectly harvested field. So then, it hadn't been an easy task after all, and her refined appearance hadn't been perfected. No doubt at least one pair of eyes had widened at the sight of her flawed womanhood—at the row of hairs that neither her hand nor her eye had reached.

She looked around in search of that pair of eyes.

It belonged to her paternal aunt, who stood looking at her with a grin on her face.

Five

Ali

༄

Dishonor doesn't die. Neither does the unnamed lover. He remains unnamed.

Among Bedouins, there are many things that don't die even if they are buried in the ground.

He observed the faces of the men who had come to offer their condolences. He scrutinized their glances, inferring whatever he could from things said and responding with a slight nod of the head to the traditional phrases of condolence. He shook the outstretched hands, feeling for a tremor or a coldness. How many Alis did he know in the line of mourners? Might "his" Ali be among them? His hand would tense up whenever he shook hands with anyone he knew, or assumed, to be an Ali.

There were bound to be plenty of Alis in a village where every boy was named after a Companion of the Prophet or one of their successors. There wasn't a single household, in fact, that didn't have an Ali, a Muhammad, a Hassan, or a Hussein, and he wasn't good at guessing which Ali belonged to which household.

Wadha and Ali, Ali and Wadha! What a conflagration the two names together had left behind! Her name had always been paired with his. "Wadha al-Mustafa"—that was what the women had called her. They didn't call her "Wadha al-Abd" (her first name followed by her father's), or "Wadha al-Salih" (her first name followed by her family name). Rather, they called her "Wadha al-Mustafa"—her first name followed by her husband's.

It was as if to say, "The woman who pleases her husband, pleases God."

Only his mother made a point of calling her by her first name followed by her family name—"Wadha al-Salih"—as if to drive home the point that no matter what her daughter-in-law did, she would always remain an outsider, an intruder: a refugee for a time. But whatever her mother-in-law's intentions were, Wadha wasn't bothered in the least.

One time, reproaching her son for not visiting her more often, she'd asked, "So who will it be: your mother or your wife? It's sure to be the one that moans with pleasure when you're on top of her!"

He laughed to himself. *Wadha is beautiful and sweet. But she doesn't moan with pleasure. If only she did!*

As he shook hands with the mourners, he noticed them prolonging the handshake, pressing their palms into his. What were they looking for? Traces of blood? The secret behind the death? Or was it an expression of schadenfreude and pity?

The wake dragged on and on. It seemed it would never end. There wasn't a man in the village who didn't shake his hand in condolence, saying, "*Salamat rasak!*"[3]

---

3   Literally, "[I pray for] your head's well-being," the colloquial phrase *salamat rasak* (*salāmat ra'sika* in standard Arabic) expresses the wish that the person who lost a loved one will enjoy safety and protection.

The laborers he transported to their work in Tel Aviv shook his hand with a nod of the head, but didn't say a word, just as they never said a word as they returned from their grueling jobs. The woman had been the focus of their conversations during work hours and breaks and before they went to sleep in their dormitory in Tel Aviv. And now she was the focus of their silent gathering.

What jobs suited the heads they carried on their shoulders? Flooring? Painting? Construction? Impregnating women with children that would turn out like their fathers? He alone was kept awake by the road, by longing, and by an angst he couldn't explain. He kept one hand on the steering wheel, and the other on the radio dial. All the songs on Friday evenings inflamed his longing for Wadha. And tonight was Friday night.

"*Ya na`im al-`oud ya siyyid al-milah!*—You with the delicate frame, the fairest of the fair ...."[4] He loved that song, though he didn't know all the words.

Whenever Wadha came to mind, he found himself immersed in the aroma of strong coffee. And whenever he took a long sip of morning coffee, a delicious tremor would go through his tongue. Wadha was like the coffee beans that danced over the fire as he stirred them lightly with the skill of an expert. As they turned browner and browner, their aroma would seep through his pores, and as he longed for the taste of the coffee, he longed for Wadha. Coffee beans require an expert, and so does a woman. The men used to chuckle and exchange winks when he bragged about his skill at preparing coffee. It was a skill that went beyond dark coffee beans.

---

4   A Kuwaiti pop song, lyrics by Ibrahim Taqi, music by Anbar bin Tirar.

After a week away from home, he'd enjoy a delicious meal and a docile woman.

Were his sleeping passengers dreaming, as he was, of a delicious meal and a docile female?

"Man," grumbled Mahmoud, a lively worker with an eye for the ladies, "we build the Jews' villas where they curse our religion. The women who live there have got it good, and they're light-skinned and delicate. And what do we get for it? We come home to grimy houses, and women who are half-dead. Where's the justice?"

Mahmoud had often gotten them in trouble with their employers because of his roving eye. As he slept, his saliva glistened around the corners of his mouth. Who was he dreaming about?

"I tell you, man, I'd give half my lifetime for a woman like Edna, the wife of that sissy who owns the house," commented Mahmoud during a work break as he licked his lips and wiped off his saliva with the edge of his sleeve.

His Wadha was prettier than Edna, he thought to himself.

"*Ya na`im al-`oud ya siyyid al-milah!*" He went back to singing the only stanza he knew of the song. He decided he'd sing it to her the next day at the eucalyptus tree she liked to sit under. She always left the huge leafy oak tree to go sit next to the eucalyptus tree instead. What was its secret, he wondered?

After preparing the slices of meat and the salad, she would get up from under the oak tree, where she'd been sitting with him and their children, to withdraw under the eucalyptus tree until he'd finished grilling the meat. As he watched her from a distance, her features would change. She would walk around the trunk, touch it, then sit down on a boulder some distance away without taking her eyes off the tree.

When she took her place beside them again, he would look into her eyes and see something that alarmed him: "Damn that eucalyptus tree! Do you worship it or something?!"

She wouldn't answer him or look him in the eye.

So one day as he was bringing the laborers back from their jobs in Tel Aviv, he pulled over and headed straight for the eucalyptus tree. They wouldn't ask him what he was doing, since half of them were asleep, and the other half weren't thinking.

He walked around to the other side of the tree, only to have his heart sink as he read: *Wadha and Ali, love forever*. Hearts had been carved into the tree trunk, and the two names side by side.

He didn't ask her about Ali, nor did she ask about the wicked fury in his eyes. She clothed herself in death, with a calmness that ill-befit a sacrificial victim.

In the mourners' faces he was searching for Ali.

Serpent

Six

Serpent

~

"What are you saying? A serpent!?"
"And not just one—there were two."
"Two? She couldn't get enough, could she?!"
"No. And not only that, but she'd tattooed it on… her backside!"
"And the second one? Please, Umm Ahmad, don't say it! Yeeee! On the… God have mercy!"
"I've been washing the dead for twenty years, and never in my life have I seen what I saw today. I swear to God, my whole body was shaking as I washed her."
"God forgive her and protect her."
"I swear, these are the end times. This is a sign of the Day of Judgment."
"Of course, Umm Ahmad, when a woman who's tattooed a serpent on her… goes to the grave… O God, don't count this against us as slander!"
"Lord have mercy! Lord have mercy! God forgive her and have mercy on all our dead."
Naeema washed the woman's corpse, trembling. Never before had she felt afraid, she who conversed regularly with death

31

in the washroom. She had always pampered it, taken care of it. Never in her twenty years of experience had a serpent shared her task with her. It was as though the colorful serpent that lay comfortably along the woman's lower back would come to life and gobble her up. As if it hadn't died, the youthful body pulsated with warmth, life, and beauty.

Another serpent lay coiled beautifully above her pubic area.

"It's the trial of the serpent. I know it. It's the test it puts everyone to—the dead and the living. It drove our forefather Adam out of Paradise. Great God forgive me. Great God forgive me! O Lord, Your protection!"

She rushed through the washing rituals, and even left some of them out. The deceased woman's sister and friend followed Naeema's instructions without much thought. Grief and sound thinking don't go together. When one shows up, the other disappears.

***

"God Almighty says in His perfect revelation: *Alluring unto man is the enjoyment of worldly desires through women, and children, and heaped-up treasures of gold and silver, and horses of high mark, and cattle, and lands. All this may be enjoyed in the life of this world – but the most beauteous of all goals is with God.*[5] Truly has God spoken.

The sheikh concluded, "Beware, O Muslims, of women's charm. Beware. They're like the serpent that lured our master Adam, peace be upon him, out of Paradise. They *are* the serpent."

---

5   Qur'an 3:14.

This was the only Quranic verse the sheikh knew. He would repeat it at wakes, where he mourned the departure of the dead and glorified death. Sometimes he would embellish it with some ready phrases and a tradition from the Prophet Muhammad. He would stumble through the tradition, only to cut it off prematurely with the words, *sadaqa rasoul Allah*— "Truly did the Messenger of God speak." But nobody ever noticed the aborted tradition or the repeated verse. Most people were too preoccupied with death's scent and shadow, while others were worrying about the meaning of existence, and the departure that lies in wait for us all.

The sheikh's voice went beyond the men's gathering to the women's, where one would shake her head, and another would purse her lips. Speaking over the sheikh, Naeema repeated over and over, "Great God, forgive me, great God, forgive me."

The deceased woman's husband looked at his watch, calculating how much longer it would be before the wake was over. It was the third day. For three days he hadn't slept a wink. If only he could doze off that night and visit her in his dreams. She'd died suddenly. Her heart had stopped, and her beautiful body had gone cold. Even the serpents that adorned it had begun to fade. Her present to him on his thirty-fifth birthday and their tenth wedding anniversary had been to tattoo a serpent at the base of her spine. A year later he had asked her to tattoo another one on her lower abdomen. She'd hesitated at first, but then she'd given in to the wishes of her husband, who found the image seductive and exciting.

Worn out by the grief and the remembering, he dozed off.

As for Naeema, she didn't sleep at all that night. As the deceased lay beautifully next to her on the bed, serpents multiplied around its edges and began to devour her.

The serpent was all the women talked about during their morning chatter sessions. It was all the men dreamt about on horny nights.

And it was Naeema's nightly companion after every death.

Soulless Cities

Seven

Soulless Cities

‍

"The first time is the killer, but nothing hurts after that. Believe me. Remove something from yourself and bury it somewhere. Then forget it."

"Like what?"

"Your fear, for example. Your shame. Your soul."

Doris would have to excise her soul, since it blocked her path every morning as she tried to drag her three children into the street. So, one morning when her children were curled up hungry in the corner of the tent, she did it. Her neighbor, a fellow refugee from her country, had died that same morning, leaving five children with a grandmother who was half dead herself, while her own children had a dead grandmother and a father who was no father at all.

She found a street corner in an elegant neighborhood where she could hunt down people's pity. She let herself and her children get filthy, taking care to keep a look of misery plastered on her face. Then she extended a timid hand which, before long, had become a bold, even brazen hand that ravished the consciences of passersby and emptied their pockets.

The coins fell one after another into her hand. Gathering them into her scarf, she slipped them into her cleavage, and by the time she got back at the end of the day, she was so fed up with the torments of hunger, she was ready to take her suffering out on everybody in the camp.

Her husband, who had started out as nothing but a distant observer, contented himself now with the role of pimp. He would send her off in the morning with a prayer for God to provide her and her children with sustenance, then roll over and go back to sleep.

By the time she'd been working the elegant street for a year and a half, Doris had learned a new language and new varieties of human death.

The next morning, she planned to gather her children and depart for distant cities. If she was lucky, she'd get a job cleaning houses, and her children might finally have a school and a house, or a house, and then a school.

She'd teach herself other skills, too.

As they boarded the train, Doris jostled other passengers trying to get a seat, and when that didn't work, she spread out with her children on the floor and fell asleep. After a couple of dreams, she woke up to find her little girl's hand outstretched and overflowing with coins.

A couple of stations later, she made sure her two little boys were covered up well. Then she took an amulet she'd smuggled out with her when she fled her country, placed it around her daughter's neck, and got off the train, light and devoid of everything.

As she struggled to recall, with her memory like quicksand, when and where she had removed her soul, she was gripped by an urgent question: Which train would take her now to soulless cities?

"All the Love
I've Known"

Eight

All the Love I've Known

∽

"We don't have girls who fall in love."

This blanket denial by the people of the village of Umm al-Zeinat might be considered shameful if its purpose weren't precisely to ward off shame and the humiliation it brings. After all, Bedouins are hospitable by nature, and have everything a guest might desire…with one exception, namely, a girl who could fall in love.

Like the title of a love poem in a school textbook, the village's name seems to suggest an invitation to enjoy beauty and tender devotion. But don't be fooled! For all the beautiful girls in the village of Umm al-Zeinat have hearts that are barren of love.

Of course, the statement "We don't have girls who fall in love" betrays the belief that girls alone bear responsibility for love, and that therefore, they alone are guilty of the sin it involves and the ignominy it brings.

The village lies nestled behind a mountain that protects it from the wind, and from the winds of passion.

If it weren't for Bedouin generosity and the sacredness of the guest—who is to be honored as though he were

41

the Prophet himself—this declaration would be written boldly at the entrance to the village. After all, God forbid that some wayfarer should think ill of its young women! And if it hadn't been for the fear of doctrinal strife, which would be worse than the taking of life itself, these same words would have been recited at the conclusion of both the obligatory and voluntary prayers. After all, it was the sacred law of the village. With it, meetings were brought to order after the mention of the Creator, and with it they were adjourned.

The only women who were trusted by the men of Umm al-Zeinat were those who had left youth and beauty behind, since there was no danger of them either causing or falling prey to temptation. They alone were assigned the task of drilling the village virgins in the sacred law: "We don't have girls who fall in love." Each of them had her own way of teaching about the evils of love, and the wolf, and the dark forest.

Like other beauties in Umm al-Zeinat, Hasna was less concerned about love than she was about asserting its absence. She resorted constantly to negations for fear of being implicated in, or even suspected of, something forbidden. Once she realized the weight of words, she lost her ability to speak easily and freely, as a girl might be killed in Umm al-Zeinat for the most harmless statement. So, she had to guard her mouth, since the most innocent slip of the tongue might mean disaster.

She avoided any term that was derived from the word "love" or even "like", and if she had no choice but to use it, she did so in the negative, as in: "I don't like to stay up late," "I don't like sweets," or "I don't like the color green."

If she was forced to choose between what she liked and what she didn't, she would force a laugh, saying, "Oh, I don't know. I don't like either one!"

When she asked herself one day what things she liked, the only answer she could come up with was that she didn't like anything at all! The realization frightened her, but at the same time, it reassured her that she was a true Bedouin.

How could she love the morning sun, and not melt in rapture over the moon by night? How could she love the taste of dew on her lips, and not be intoxicated by an imagined kiss? What devil could promise her that if she loved the shadows of dusk, she wouldn't swoon over some shepherd who made his way into her dawn hours? And every night, Umm Kulthum would make her virgin cheeks blush as she listened to her on the radio during the men's gatherings, singing: "All the love I've known, I've known through you, and all the years I've lived, I've lived for you!"

"Sing it, woman, sing it!" one of the men would shout rapturously.

These men would welcome Umm Kulthum into their gatherings, then take in her words with their coffee, their cigarettes and their muffled gasps. Isn't singing love's praises the same as love itself in our men's book? But the rules that apply to the girls of Umm al-Zeinat don't apply to Umm Kulthum.

Warda, the prettiest girl in the village, had a lovely voice. The other girls would gather around her among the almond trees as she sang, "All the love I've known, I've known through you, and all the years I've lived, I've lived for you."

"Warda's in love," they whispered to each other.

Warda had been pretty all along, but now she was prettier. The *wadi* echoed the sound of her laughter. But then she disappeared, and with her, her sweet voice.

Another one that disappeared was Noura, with the black eyes and the long lashes. One morning she'd been pasturing the sheep and the goats, but the dusk swallowed her up, and she never returned. Her mother cried, but the women scolded her. Then they stopped taking their daughters to Noura's house.

Dalal disappeared too. Her mother didn't cry. They said her brother was a man, and that this was how men were supposed to be in Umm al-Zeinat.

Hasna hated her village, and she hated its law: "We don't have girls who fall in love." In Umm al-Zeinat, a girl who fell in love got prettier, and her laughter would ring out. Then she would go live in the sky. She would only visit the village in her mother's nightmares, and sometimes her ghost would steal into the almond grove, but her voice would remain muted.

Hasna dreamed that she had black eyes and long, silky hair that touched the ground. She was singing in the almond grove, "All the love I've known, I've known through you, and all the years I've lived, I've lived for you." Her voice was beautiful, as if it belonged to somebody else. She sang and sang until all the almonds fell to the ground.

The next morning, she took the herd of sheep and goats out to pasture, and before the gloom of evening had found its way to the houses in the village, she came down the mountain, leaving the herd behind. She whispered in her little sister's ear, "Drive the herd back to the house. I'm going to look for a village where girls don't disappear if they sing and fall in love."

The girl grew up and forgot her older sister. Then she dreamed about the almond grove, and long hair, and Umm Kulthum, and she remembered that she had a sister who had gone looking...for love.

Umm Kulthum's
Intercessor

Nine

Umm Kulthum's Intercessor

⌐

"You shameless brat!"

I was sixteen years old, and she was sixty-one. It was the only time she'd ever slapped me on the cheek, and it rang in my ears for days. It was followed by a thunderous scream that hurt me as though she'd slapped me a second time: "Now get out of my face!"

It was also the only time she'd kicked me out of her room. Even though I didn't bear her name and I wasn't the oldest of her eight grandchildren, I was her favorite granddaughter. From the time I was little until that night, she'd been accustomed to calling me "Habiba," or "Beloved." When she called me from her room, she didn't need to mention my name. It was enough for her to say, "Come here, Habiba!" and everybody in the house would know I was the one intended. Everybody else in the big house had names she called them by, and sometimes the name would be followed by an identification of how they were related to her. It was as if, when she asked them for something, she wanted to remind them of her rights over them, and their duty towards her.

47

I came out of her room, my palm covering my humiliated cheek, and hid in my room before anyone in the house noticed my fall from grace. Once the incident was noted, it would beg the urgent, disapproving question: "What happened?" Then they would present a list of hypotheses for me to choose from, possibly with just a nod of the head. But none of that happened. She retreated for refuge into her prayers and pleas for God's forgiveness, and I, into my books and my silence.

However, there was another 'Habiba' whose name was distinguished from mine by the two Arabic letters *alif* and *lam*, or the definite article 'the'. This other person was "*al*-Habiba", or "*The* Beloved," whereas I was just "Habiba."

Despite my youth and my ignorance of the rules that governed definite and indefinite articles and the weight that was carried by the former, I was terribly jealous of that other "Habiba." My childlike intuition told me I was the loser in an unnamed game whose outcome had been determined before I was born, and that any attempt on my part to reverse that outcome was bound to fail. After all, I was competing against a woman I knew nothing about but her name, her voice, and the times when she came on the radio or television—times which, to Grandma, were sacred. At some point in my life, I made peace with this defeat, reminding myself that among all those my grandmother loved, I enjoyed the singular honor of being second only to Umm Kulthum.

The voice of Umm Kulthum, the beloved Prima Donna (and, as the people in our household referred to her, *habibat al-jadda*, or Grandma's Beloved) would emanate from the eastern room at specific times of day. We arranged our schedules around this and could predict our grandmother's mood based on her song selections. It was a voice rivaled (albeit weakly) only by that of the reciter on the Qur'an radio station, which my grandmother would listen to for an hour every day after the dawn prayer. If, on a given day, she granted the reciter a more generous share of time than she did to The Beloved, the "imbalance" could be explained by the fact that our grandmother wanted to commemorate someone who had died, or she'd had a bad dream, or people had suffered some unforeseen disaster. In other cases, it might be on account of some inadvertent sin she'd committed, or an urgent request she needed to bring before her Creator and which called for a lengthy Qur'an recitation followed by a session of praise and pleas for forgiveness on her prayer beads.

Umm Kulthum's voice was one I didn't know how to classify or describe with my limited 8-year-old vocabulary. It wasn't pretty, and it wasn't ugly. It wasn't smooth, and it wasn't gravelly. It wasn't comforting, and it wasn't irritating. It was just Umm Kulthum's voice, as my grandmother would say. In my view, this placed it outside the realm of all classification, and in my grandmother's view, above all classification. As far as she was concerned, it was sui generis.

She would exclaim, "Isn't it a shame for a woman with a voice like that to be six feet under the ground? I swear, it's a crying shame!"

Then, with the fear of a believer who's just caught herself committing some terrible transgression, she would exclaim, "Lord, forgive me!"

Her children and grandchildren knew how to appease her if she was irritated or tap her generous side if she was feeling stingy. When we wanted something, we'd appeal either to her Lord, or to her Beloved. If we begged her, "For your Beloved's sake, Grandma!" she would chuckle and give us whatever we asked for. Slipping her hand under the pillow, she'd pull out her black leather wallet, take out 20-pound notes and distribute them among us equally. Then she'd wink at me, and I'd shoo them all out of the room with my finger on my mouth, saying, "Sh-h-h-h-h-h! It's about time for Umm Kulthum to come on the radio!" Then I'd sneak back in for another 20-pound note and rush out again before anybody noticed.

On her 60th birthday, I spent a whole day waiting in the gift shop near my school while the shop owner worked on arranging a legendary encounter between my grandmother and Umm Kulthum. I'd brought him two pictures, one of my grandmother, and the other of Umm Kulthum. The picture of my grandmother showed her at a family wedding wearing the embroidered dress she always saved for weddings and holidays, sitting happily with her hands crossed over her chest and watching the celebration, while the one of Umm Kulthum showed her on stage in that famous stance of hers: handkerchief in hand, arms raised heavenward, and her mouth open wide in a prolonged "ah".

"That's the best I can do!" said the shop owner after hours in front of the computer screen, cutting and adding, enlarging and reducing, moving images farther apart and closer together.

"No, no," I said, "my grandmother's too far away. Could you bring her closer to Umm Kulthum, please?," "Please make the picture in color," and "My grandmother doesn't seem to be looking at Umm Kulthum."

Then at long last, I saw Umm Kulthum standing directly in front of my grandmother as though she were singing to her alone, while my grandmother sat with her hands clasped over her bosom, an audience of one entranced by the majesty of the Prima Donna.

When she saw the picture for the first time, my grand-mother gasped and nearly fainted. "God have mercy!" she muttered as she wiped her face with her hands. She gawked at the picture, rubbing her eyes in disbelief and giggling like a little girl who's woken on the Eid to find a new dress waiting for her. I explained to her that technology can work miracles, such as collapsing distances, transcending time and place, im-mortalizing the departed, and joining them with the living in photographs that look convincingly real. Once she'd gained her composure, she told me she'd dreamed about being at an Umm Kulthum concert, and that when she saw the picture, she'd felt confused, not knowing whether she was still dream-ing, or if the dream had come true.

She studied it at length, running her fingers over the faces under the glass. Then, pointing to the wall in front of her, she said, "Hang it there to the left of the verse." She was referring to a framed verse from the Quran, written in Kufic script, which had been given to her by a beggar that roamed the village with framed Quranic verses in his left hand, and with his right hand outstretched to the charitable as he prayed for God to grant them protection and prosperity. The verse read: *His is the dominion of the heavens and the earth. He gives life and deals death, and He has power over all things.*[6]

---

6   The verse is Qur'an 2:225, referred to popularly as the Throne Verse, which reads: *God - there is no deity except Him, the Ever-Living, the Self-Sustaining. Neither drowsiness overtakes Him nor sleep. To Him belongs whatever is in the heavens and whatever is on the earth. Who is it that can intercede with Him except by His permis-sion? He knows what is [presently] before them and what will be after them, and they encompass not a thing of His knowledge except for what He wills. His Throne extends over the heavens and the earth, and their preservation tires Him not. And He is the Most High, the Most Great.*

Thus, the picture came to rest next to the verse on the wall directly across from her bed. Now there were two images and two certainties that had been joined in her heart, so if doubt crept in concerning one of them, the second would come and drive it out. The first certainty was the dominion of the Lord of the Worlds over all things, and the second was her having met face to face with The Beloved, Umm Kulthum (the truth of the matter being known only to her clever granddaughter and the owner of Maher's Gift Shop).

Staring at the picture in consternation, the few village women who came to see her were convinced that she'd been hiding the secret of her having attended an Umm Kulthum concert once upon a time, ignoring the facts of death and life, the difference in eras, and the geographical distances that would have easily toppled her claim.

"Tell us about it!" they urged eagerly.

She explained to them proudly that her diligent teenage granddaughter was a "genie," that science could now work miracles, and that they hadn't seen anything yet. One of them would imagine a picture of herself blowing a kiss to Abdel Halim Hafez,[7] while another (as long as technology was capable of such miraculous feats) would soar on the wings of imagination to a film showing her wrapping her arms around Rushdy Abaza[8] and singing to him demurely, `Ashi'a wa Ghalbana wa-n-nabi.[9]

---

7   Abdel Halim Hafez (1929-1977) was an Egyptian singer, actor and conductor.

8   Rushdy Abaza (1926-1980) was an Egyptian actor.

9   Literally, "In Love and Victorious, I swear by the Prophet!", `Āshi'a wa Ghalbāna wa-n-Nabī is the name of a popular song performed by Sabah (1937-2014), lyrics by Muhammad Hamza (1969-).

Another person who fell for the story was the neighbor lady across the street who, standing on her terrace, called out to my grandmother at the top of her lungs, "Hey there, Umm Umar, I swear by the Qur'an and the Most Merciful, the song where Umm Kulthum sings, 'with confident steps, he walks like a king'[10] comes straight into my house. Does it come into yours?"

Smiling, my grandmother looked at her from the window of her room and replied, "No, it doesn't."

Radio in hand, the neighbor lady gave a triumphant flick of the head. Then she turned the volume up full blast so the whole neighborhood could hear that Umm Kulthum's voice had graced her house alone with the words, "with confident steps, he walks like a king", and that even Umm Umar's house had been passed by! Umm Umar would never have forgiven anybody who claimed to have a monopoly on Umm Kulthum except for the fact that this particular neighbor lady was poor as a church mouse and weak in the head, facts which ranked her among those unfortunate souls whose trespasses are forgiven, and who might even be classed as saints if their trespasses are occasioned by a passion for Umm Kulthum.

When the neighbor lady stood dumbfounded in front of the picture of Umm Umar and Umm Kulthum, my grandmother made little effort to explain to her the miracles of science and technology. After all, if this poor woman's mental capacities were so limited that she thought her radio was the only one that picked up Umm Kulthum's songs, she was sure to believe that Umm Kulthum and my grandmother really *could* appear in the same picture. It wouldn't hurt for there to be somebody

---

10 A phrase from the song entitled, 'The Ruins" (*al-Aṭlāl*), lyrics by Ibrahim Naji, music by Riad Al Sunbati, 1990.

besides my grandmother who believed in this possibility. Even so, she could never have imagined what impact this marvel would have on the poor woman. She no longer poked her head out her window to announce loudly which song Umm Kulthum was singing on a given evening. In fact, I don't think she even listened to her anymore. Instead, she would go back and forth across the street between her house and ours, steadying her radio on her left shoulder while she fiddled with the radio dial, but without settling on one station.

As she passed under my grandmother's window, she would shout, "Umm Umar stole Umm Kulthum from our radio. I swear by the Qur'an and the Most Merciful, I saw Umm Kulthum at her house!"

For days after this, my grandmother reproached herself for the unintended setback she'd caused this neighbor. Fearful that her "sin" would strap her with a debt, she set about repaying it by doubling her prayers and prolonging her other religious observances the way she did whenever she owed an earthly debt. As she always reminded her children, "We shouldn't make other people pay for our mistakes." Eventually, the neighbor lady stopped picking fights with my grandmother every day the way she had been. This was a sign my grandmother had been waiting for, so her conscience was relieved, and she went back to her milder penance regimens.

"The first time I met the Prima Donna was more than thirty years ago," she reminisced. "I went with your grandfather - God bless his soul – to Haifa to visit Ezra, the man in charge of the village's forests. Your grandfather went to ask him to release a herd of goats that had been confiscated on the pretext that he'd been grazing them in protected areas. While we were going there on the bus, he told me just to return their greeting, and not say another word. When we got there, we all sat in the living room. Ezra's busybody wife sat next me, screwing up her mouth and eavesdropping on the men's conversation. On the television screen in front of me stood the Prime Donna, singing, 'What can I tell you about longing?' I don't know how long I sat there with my eyes and ears glued to the screen, but after a while I heard Ezra brag, 'I attended a concert of hers in Baghdad in 1946. I was in the front row!'

"I cursed him in my heart. How was it that this man and his crooked-mouthed wife got the chance to see and hear Umm Kulthum, but I didn't? On our way back, I asked your grandfather if Umm Kulthum had ever sung in Haifa, and he snapped angrily, 'What did we come out to do, anyway? To find out about Umm Kulthum, or the herd of goats we're about to lose!?'"

I used to call them "bathroom stories," since they came enveloped in the scent of soap and the mist left by the hot water. She would trim her hair and pour water over her hair and body, while my job was to wash her hair, rub her back and listen to the details of whatever story she was telling. I used to prolong the bathroom ritual, hoping to pick up on details that were for my ears only.

"He was harsh, gruff, and jealous, God forgive him! He used to monopolize the radio, even though the only things he listened to were the news and rebab music. If he caught me listening to Umm Kulthum and humming along, he'd blow up. Then he started taking it with him to the pasture during the day. He was suspicious by nature and used to say the only people who listened to Umm Kulthum were lovers. But he's rested from his labors now and given me a rest from him!"

It wasn't just Umm Kulthum's voice, or the picture of them together, that would put a happy twinkle in my grandmother's eye, but every piece of news or information that reinforced her conviction that Umm Kulthum was a legend not only as a singer, but in all aspects of her life. I used to go hunting for tidbits about her in the newspapers or on websites I found on the school computer. After a while, it became such a treat that if a week went by without my bringing her anything new, she would feel as though something was missing. So sometimes I would repeat old news, and she would listen to it as enthusiastically as she had the first time she heard it. My haul of news items tended to be especially generous on the anniversaries of her birthday or death, when the newspapers would publish rare photos, secrets, and details that revealed more and more about her life. I used to divide these up over the days to satisfy my grandmother's appetite for Umm Kulthum trivia, and in hopes of enjoying those looks of contentment and approval in her eyes.

I also used to rephrase and edit some of the news to bring it into line with her biases. I might suggest, for example, that if it hadn't been for Umm Kulthum, composers and writers like Riad Al Sunbati, Ahmed Rami, Zakariyya Ahmad and Baligh Hamdi wouldn't have risen to prominence. Or I might exaggerate and say they were all madly in love with her and were dying to win her approval, speculations she would affirm with an enthusiastic nod of the head.

Sometimes I introduced the news with leading questions and watched her eyes get big, ready to devour the answers to follow.

"Do you know why she wears sunglasses?" I asked, "Or why she holds a handkerchief when she sings? Or when she visited Palestine? Did you know she started out as a Qur'an reciter, and turned to singing later? And that until she was ten years old, she dressed up as a boy?"

She shook her head in pleased astonishment.

"Did you know she quit singing after Abdel Nasser died, but Anwar Sadat persuaded her to go back to it?"

At this she drew a deep breath.

"Did you know she was the first female lead musician?"

Here she took an even deeper breath, swelling visibly with pride.

"And that she played a major role in the campaign to rearm the Egyptian army after the defeat of '67 by giving concerts all over the world and donating her entire proceeds to the war effort?"

By this time, she was beside herself with delight.

The prelude to the song *hajartak*—"I've left you"—had begun. During the long instrumental introductions that preceded Umm Kulthum's songs, we could exchange a word or two with my grandmother. But from the moment she uttered the first word of the song until she "left the stage," as my grandmother put it, all conversation was forbidden. If we made the slightest sound, she would scold us and threaten us with dire consequences, or glare at us until we shut our mouths and left her room.

It was a sacred time, and to get the point across to us, she would say, "There are two things you should never interrupt: my prayers, and my hour of rapture!"

After serious thought, we concluded from this comparison that just as *du'a' al-istighfar*, or the traditional plea for forgiveness, concluded my grandmother's ritual prayers, Umm Kulthum's "leaving the stage" concluded her hour of rapture. Nobody was permitted to talk until after that time.

We could see with our own eyes when our grandmother had folded up her prayer rug, hung her prayer beads around her neck, and sat down on her chair or bed, so we would know it was alright to talk again. But we couldn't figure out how we were supposed to know when Umm Kulthum had left the stage. After all, nobody could see her on the radio!

We tried to calculate, or at least guess, how long the stage was, how many steps led down from it, and how nimbly Umm Kulthum could navigate them given the fact that she was around my grandmother's age. In the end, we concluded that the average time she would need to come down from the stage after finishing her performance would be around the same as it took my grandmother to recite the plea for forgiveness and the formulas of praise after her ritual prayer.

"Sh-h-h-h … I don't want to hear a peep out of you!"

"What time is it? In half an hour, Umm Kulthum comes on."

"I swear to God, there's no other voice like yours, my Beloved!"

Words like these taught us never to interrupt either her prayer or her hour of rapture.

Then one day, on the anniversary of Umm Kulthum's death, a certain secret was revealed by a newspaper with evidence from Umm Kulthum's life to back up the claim. Namely, that my grandmother's Beloved had preferred women over men, as it were. This startling piece of information dogged me all the way home from school, and all the way up to my grandmother's room that night. I hesitated to tell her about it. This was no ordinary piece of news. On the contrary, it was scandalous enough that it would confuse my grandmother at best, and at worst, make her furious with the newspapers. But when I walked into her room and saw the peaceful look on her face as she listened to the introduction to the song of the evening, I settled the matter in my mind.

At long last, the old childish envy of Umm Kulthum had found an outlet in a tidbit of disagreeable news that would flip the equation.

It was the old defeat that I'd never accepted.

So I started reading the news items just as they'd been reported in the newspaper, pausing as usual between one sentence and the next to make sure she was listening, and in anticipation of an admiring nod of the head or a satisfied gleam in the eye. However, her hand was swifter than either her head or her eye, and it landed full force on my cheek with the words, "You shameless brat!"

Tripping repeatedly over my shamelessness, I stumbled out of her room and into my own while avoiding contact with anyone else in the house. I tripped over it again whenever someone wondered aloud about the reason for my grandmother's isolation and the absence of Umm Kulthum's voice from her room. Her children were afraid her sudden loss of interest in anything but solitary fasting, praying and pleas for divine forgiveness might be a sign of impending death, since the forty days before a person dies are accompanied by cryptic signs observed by this person alone, such as recurring nightmares of an open grave.

I was less preoccupied with the imminent death others had been speculating about than I was with another fear, namely, that my grandmother would die sad, or leave this world with anger in her heart towards me or Umm Kulthum. More specifically, I was preoccupied with a wish I'd once promised to fulfill for her.

One night after Umm Kulthum had "come down from the stage" (I don't remember the song she sang that night), my grandmother had whispered to me that when she died and the three days of mourning were over, she wanted me to make sure Umm Kulthum's voice went on being heard in the house at her sacred times. She said she wanted it to be a kind of ongoing charity, given on her behalf to people in the household and passers-by.

But was this still my grandmother's wish now that Umm Kulthum had abandoned her room while she was still among the living?

After that slap I entered her room only rarely, and when I did, I made sure our eyes didn't meet. I was avoiding that mysterious thing that gleamed in her eyes and that had stuck in my memory since that night, erasing all the cherished looks of joy, contentment, and reassurance. She also made sure our eyes didn't meet, though I don't know what she was avoiding. I would set her fast-breaking meal on her little table before the sundown call to prayer, or gather her dry clothes from the clothesline, arrange them in her closet, and make a quick exit.

But one day as I was on my way out, an amazing thing happened.

I noticed that there wasn't a trace of my grandmother in the picture on the wall. As I crossed the two-meter distance between the closet and the door, I tried to find her, opening my eyes as wide as they'd go and scrutinizing the picture in detail. But all I could see was Umm Kulthum and her audience looking out at me from a black and white picture, an ordinary picture no different from hundreds of others I'd seen.

My grandmother wasn't there.

My eyes weren't lying, and neither was the picture.

I remembered the "weak-minded" neighbor lady, who appeared to have the kind of supernatural powers enjoyed by saints and other blessed souls. She must have expelled Umm Kulthum from my grandmother's radio, then caused a rift between me and my grandmother, and between my grandmother and Umm Kulthum. And now she was completing the punishment by concealing my grandmother from the picture. Did I dare ask other people in the house to look at the picture and help me figure out whether my grandmother had really left it, or whether she'd been in it to start with?

There was no way I was going to ask my grandmother why she'd withdrawn from the picture.

But after forty days of solitude and worship, I heard her voice coming out of her room one evening.

Laughing serenely, she called out, "Come here, Habiba!"

I didn't believe my ears until the call came again: "Come here, Habiba!"

Seated on the edge of the bed, she was drying her long hair with a towel, then letting it cascade gently over her shoulders and thighs. Making a half-turn, she extended the comb in my direction as if to say, "Come, comb my hair." Her hands still nimble, she worked the tangles out of her long curly hair and divided it evenly into two large bunches which she then turned into a pair of thick braids that met in the form of a sated snake that lay curled up at the back of her head.

I began braiding her hair. Then, unable to contain myself, I asked her, "Grandma, have you forgiven me?"

She made no reply. Instead, she asked for her embroidered dress, put it on, then wrapped her head in her white shawl stitched with golden threads and sat down in the middle of her bed. She asked me what time it was. Then, moving the radio dial with the skill of the blind, she put it on her favorite station. In a barely audible voice, the announcer was finishing the news summary.

She sat up straight, bringing the radio closer to her. Then, pointing towards the wall, she said suddenly, "Damn it all, that picture's still crooked, Habiba!"

The chair that sat against the wall directly below the tilted picture bore the footprints of an unsuccessful attempt to straighten it. Standing on the chair, I moved the frame left and right according to my grandmother's instructions until the picture hung straight.

As I was getting down off the chair, she said suddenly, "Can you check for me to see if I'm back in the picture, Habiba?"

"Yes, you're there, Grandma," I assured her.

And there she was, her hands crossed over her chest, decked out in her colorful embroidered dress and ready to belt out enthusiastic cries of approval. Forty days of seclusion and worship had paved the way for a long life to come, both inside and outside the picture.

Dear listeners, until the time of the news broadcast an hour from now, we leave you with Umm Kulthum's song of the night: Ansak (I'll Forget You), lyrics by poet Mamoun Al-Shinnawi and music by Baligh Hamdi. We wish you an enjoyable hour.

As usual, she turned the volume dial two complete revolutions so that everybody in the house, the neighbors, and passers-by could all hear the song of the evening.

Once the instrumental prelude was over, I returned the chair to its place. With one hand I gently closed the door, and with the other, I nudged out of the room a protesting crowd that I'd pulled out of the picture.

"More, Madame, more!" they cried.

"Sh-h-h-h-h-h-h," I whispered, my finger to my mouth.

A Funny
Red Rose

Ten

A Funny Red Rose

A lonely woman with a funny red rose in her hair, she sat in the restaurant where the couple had eaten two years earlier.

With her smart phone she was filming a chef as he showed customers his extraordinary skill at "dancing" with food and fire, while other restaurant goers, both tourists and locals, were filming the woman and the chef.

"Shall I pour the wine for two, Madame?" the waiter asked.

"Of course," she replied. "He should be here any moment now."

He poured the wine and didn't ask about the other person. He'd stopped marveling over people who were there but couldn't be seen. After twenty years at the restaurant, and a few elsewhere, he had learned that the people he didn't see must be there.

The woman ate with the greatest of elegance. The next day she would be returning to her house in Vienna. But she was still worried about her garden. The roses were quick to wilt. He used to manage to take care of them even when the two of them were away, and they would be lush and beautiful even after a week's absence.

Would they still be that way now? Lush and beautiful? Nothing was the way it had been, herself included. Her sorrow over his absence had become as pleasantly familiar as her pillow, and over her morning coffee she would carry on calm, polite conversations with the longing for his presence.

She also used to visit him every month. She would tell him everything he liked to hear and didn't like to hear.

"John," she said, "you know I don't much like the color black. I threw out all my mourning clothes. You yourself used to laugh at traditions of mourning, didn't you?

"Now, can I tell you something? I didn't really like all the red roses you used to pick for me from our garden. If you'd only brought me a yellow one or a white one, even just once! But not to worry. The important thing is that you went painlessly. I pick red roses for your sake, to bring them here. I'm traveling tomorrow, and I won't be coming here again. This is the last time. I'm saying goodbye, John. Take care of yourself, my dear."

As she pulled her heavy bag along in the distance, she glimpsed her neighbor coming out of her garden and closing its low gate behind him. He smiled at her and raised his hand in greeting. As she climbed the steps leading up to her house, she was awaited by a large vase filled with yellow and white roses.

She took one and placed it in her hair before opening the door to go inside.

She laughed, saying, "I'm a lonely woman with a funny yellow rose in my hair."

Bride

Eleven

Bride

⦿

A huge oak tree split our path, and our childhood, in two: what came before the tree, and what came after it.

As we've counted the steps and the years, it's receded into history. It's become a sacred tree redolent with the fragrances of manly, aged incense.

The tree stood in the middle of our path: behind it lay closely packed houses, and in front of it ran a narrow street.

It was an enormous oak tree well-suited to be haunted by jinn and lied about by adults. During the day we would tiptoe around the lies, and at night we'd fear the jinn. We escaped from them, but they remained trapped in our forebodings.

As for the lies, they destroyed two childhoods and a swing.

A bride was late for her wedding. She'd been dyeing her new notebook with leftover henna, and she'd written her name on it in slanted Kufic script. Ululating, her mother's neighbor drew two hearts and two initials on the back of her petite hand.

The bride's younger sister then tore up the notebook and made its pages into paper airplanes that would barely fly.

Another bride was delighted with a white dress that her mother had taken off one of her dolls. When the gathering dispersed, the dress caught on fire and she discovered that the tiresome holiday guest hadn't been a holiday guest after all, and that her white dress wasn't as pretty as she'd thought it was. She took off running through the night and the trees ran with her, barefoot.

I used to think the giant oak tree was the arm of God. I hid under it, but I was discovered by a wandering eye. How was it, I wondered incredulously, that the arm of God hadn't protected me?

A certain uncle said, "God lives in the tree and moves the wind, but He doesn't ignite wars."

A muddle-headed grandfather said, "God goes away in the summer, leaving us the fast, and a sun that doesn't budge from its place."

A certain mother whose little girl had run away one night (and with her, a forest) burned down the oak tree, saying it was possessed by a demon.

As they were burying the tree, everybody said a demon had possessed the poor mother.

w - h - o - r - e

Twelve

W - h - o - r - e

$\backsim$

"We should go for a family outing to the Jaffa beach. They say it's great. What do you say, brother?"

"Who says it's so great? Has that sister of ours been passing on some of her slutty ideas? Or are you just covering up for her?"

"Actually, they say it's a lovers' beach, and as far as I can tell, we've passed the lovers' phase. Or would you disagree?"

He didn't really care what she thought. He just wanted to detect some tension in her voice, or a wary glance over at their sister that might betray some of what the two women were hiding. He was sure she'd cover up for their sister and her lies. Was he destined to bear the disgrace of the women in his family, even if it was only potential or anticipated?

He envied his neighbor, Abu Tariq. Abu Tariq didn't have any sisters or paternal aunts, and his children were all boys. So where would the disgrace come from? When Abu Tariq swore by his honor, he didn't have to worry about anybody giving him a sideways glance. As for him, he avoided swearing by anything but God and His most beautiful names. When he wanted to stress a point, he would gesture with his hand, saying, "By God, and His majesty and power!" which imbued his oaths with an air of sanctity.

"So what's wrong with that?" she countered. "Aren't you in love with your wife? And aren't I in love with my husband?"

"And our little sister? Is she in love with somebody too? The Jaffa beach with its breeze is a perfect place for love, and other things..."

Do you suppose she's still a virgin? God forbid that she.....!

He started with fright. Seeing drops of blood in his path, he swerved to avoid them, and nearly fell on his face.

"What's wrong, brother? It's still early. The party hasn't started yet!"

Early?!

It might be quite late. Too late. He was done for. Done for.

When had this fixation come over him? And was it just an obsession, or a reality?

A statement he'd heard somebody make—was it the sheikh in one of his sermons? Or maybe a religious friend of his? He couldn't remember exactly—had triggered an obsession with dishonor. He was so scared, it was all he could think about. Had the person who made the statement been addressing him in particular? Or had he been talking about reforming society by dealing with immoral women in general? Were other men making jokes about him behind his back?

As the saying goes, "If a girl spends the night away from home, break a jar over her head." That means every girl, and any girl.

Their little sister had been sleeping away from home ever since she started studying at Tel Aviv University. What use was a university degree if it meant a spoiled reputation?

He'd heard stories of lovers who came to the beach under cover of darkness to escape people's prying eyes. For all he knew, his little sister who'd been spending her nights in Tel Aviv might be one of them. What was to prevent her?

"We can't wait to go to the beach and spend an evening there. Why can't we be like everybody else?"

At last, he gave in to the pleas of his wife and children, and before long they were packing a picnic, ready for an evening on the beach. Nobody could have guessed what he was thinking.

He lit the fire to grill the meat, then left the remaining tasks to his wife and children. As everybody else got busy grabbing whatever limited enjoyment they could while the night lasted, he sat peering like a spy into the shadows.

Amorous couples were taking refuge in the surrounding darkness.

He scrutinized people's faces but could barely make out their features. After all, these lovers were fleeing from sight in the dark corners that couldn't be reached by the dim lamps overhead.

Then he glimpsed her from a distance. It was her. He knew it. He recognized her walk, and her silhouette. He would recognize her even in the darkness and from behind.

He began to reel. But he was determined not to fall. Not yet.

Get a hold of yourself. Get a hold of yourself.

The young man had one hand around her waist, and the other on her belly.

Get a hold of yourself. Don't you dare fall until you've grabbed her by her headscarf and dragged her to the car. The guy's not your concern now. Surprise her from behind and haul her away like a stubborn sheep.

75

"I swear, I'll strangle you with my own hands and bury you at the edge of town, you whore.

"You whore.

"You w ... h ..."

***

Her hand caressed his head, and a tear fell onto his face.

"Where am I?"

"You're all right, brother. You're all right."

Hadn't he killed her?

His wife glared at him furiously.

"What came over you, man? How could you attack a pregnant woman that way? What did you expect? Did you really think her husband and her brother would keep quiet about something like that? Be thankful they didn't kill you!"

"Now's not the time for that," chided his (*w ... h ... o ... r ... e*) of a sister. "All that matters now is that he's okay."

"But she looked like her. She looked a lot like her," he murmured inaudibly before drifting to sleep.

The Door
to the
Body

Thirteen

The Door to the Body

 ✐

For two weeks Selma had been eavesdropping through the flimsy wall, following developments in a debate between her parents over whether to send her to a boarding school. She hadn't been able to make out most of the details, especially the ones relating to the reasons for the action being proposed. She hadn't heard a word about the virtues of the nuns' system, or their role in refining and educating young girls. Rather, the whole conversation focused on her and her body: what others saw, how they saw it, and certain senses that might be awakened by a body as it grew.

Whenever her parents disagreed on whatever it was that would necessitate transferring her to a boarding school, they would lower their voices to a whisper.

In her father's view, a certain pair of something-or-others had gotten large enough to be noticeable to the truck drivers who came down the road that flanked the village every morning, whereas according to her mother, they were barely visible from under her brassiere. In fact, they just barely showed when she took the brassiere off and tossed it onto the nearest chair. (She still hadn't gotten used to having a piece of cloth confine her youthful body, and she would slip it off deftly from under her school uniform so that she could get a breath.)

Even so, her father swore he'd seen a truck slow down as a sleepy, horny-looking driver leaned out the window and watched a girl rushing to the bus station. If it hadn't been for the morning fog, you could have seen him drooling, he said.

"Don't you fear God, woman? When we're looking the other way, somebody might come along and seduce her, and something terrible would happen!"

In a coarse whisper, Selma's mother instructed her to keep her breasts from getting any larger and rounder until her father calmed down. Meanwhile, she worked to stave off all her husband's attempts to send their daughter away to a school that was basically nothing but a shelter for orphans and the unfortunate.

"What would people say?" the mother argued back. "That we don't know how to raise our daughter? I mean, really! Is she an orphan?"

Selma wasn't actually that bothered by the thought of going to the boarding school. She didn't know much about it, although she had heard it was strict, and that the treatment was harsh.

What bothered her most was her parents' preoccupation with a part of her body that didn't even mean much to her. She didn't see it as a hindrance, and definitely not as something to drool over!

One day she asked her best friend Nisreen, "Hasn't your dad ever thought of sending you to a boarding school?"

"Why would he do that?"

"Well, how big are your boobs? I mean, what bra size do you wear?"

"What's wrong with you?" Nisreen shot back. "Have you lost your mind? First you ask about a boarding school, and then you ask about my bra size. What's the connection?"

"I don't know. But my dad seems to think there is one."

What Selma had just said might have spelled the end of their friendship if it hadn't been for the fact that she followed it with a hysterical laugh that made Nisreen think she'd just been joking.

For weeks on end she tried to arrive at some logical rule or equation that would connect girls' breast sizes with their education. She spent more time than usual looking at herself in the mirror and running her hands over her body.

Pondering her breasts, she tried to come up with something she could compare them to. The one that came to mind made her laugh. One of her aunts used to pick tomatoes from a family garden and divide them up based on their sizes. The biggest ones went in one box, the medium-sized ones in another box, and the smallest ones in a third box.

The Sister will take all the new girls in the school and line us up in a row. Then she'll sort us the way my aunt sorts tomatoes. I might end up in the medium-sized group. Ha ha ha! Who knows?

The only person Selma knew who lived in a boarding school was a girl named Buthayna. Buthayna's parents had died and her brothers' wives had gotten tired of taking care of her. So it had been decided that the best solution was to have her live away from the family. She attended regular school in the morning, and in the afternoon she went back to the boarding school. The white blouse she wore was so loose, you couldn't tell whether she'd been sent to the boarding school on account of her bra size, or because of her family tragedy.

Buthayna didn't talk or smile much. But everybody said that was just her nature, and that it had nothing to do with the evening prison.

Then one morning, the tragedy was completed, or ended.

Buthayna disappeared. According to the girls at school, she'd run away with the truck driver who used to transport things she needed to the nuns' school. He'd seduced her, and she'd taken off with him.

Selma took the news back to her mother. The evening was enveloped in silence. This was the first sign of victory.

Her father closed the door to the boarding school idea once and for all.

As for Selma, she opened another door: the door to a relationship with her body. Her own body.

Barbed Question

Fourteen

Barbed Question

✑

" *Wayn, ya m'sahhil?* Where you off to, wanderer?"
It's either a question that conceals a prayer, or a prayer that conceals a wily question.

On one level, it's a perfectly innocent query that employs a figure of speech in its original and derived meanings alike.[11] It's addressed to the hurried guest, urging him or her to stay and expressing disappointment over their hasty departure. It's also flung at a female passerby, who immediately goes in search of a reply, an escape, or a wall to hide behind or beat her head up against.

If a woman or girl manages to get past the village's male gathering—whether by crawling like a snake, running like a sheepdog, or evaporating like their cigarette smoke—and if the barbed question, "*Wayn, ya m'sahhil?*" doesn't grab her by the hem of her dress or the tip of her braid, she'll be ready to face anything. She'll be prepared to cross the street, ford rivers and streams, penetrate the very sky.

---

11 The word *m'sahhil* (*musahhil*) is derived from a prayer often addressed to someone leaving on a journey: *Allāh yusahhil `alayk*, meaning, "May God make [your path] smooth, or easy for you."

On the bus going to Haifa, she may look dully at the other passengers, making sure they see her and that she isn't a phantom. Between Haifa's Abbas Street and Wadi al-Nasnas, she'll draw a fine line that would make her the envy of feminists and female revolutionaries.

It's a line she's already paid the price for, or that she'll pay for later once her revolution has subsided.

If the question hit its target and she's found no wall to hide behind, she'll stifle the reply and bury it along with amulets for attracting a beloved or driving out jinn, then go back to where she came from.

The attempts to prevent her getaway are never-ending. Most of them bounce off, though some hit their mark.

Those who've been accustomed to being imprisoned in a hut but stick their head out a small window to steal a look around or a breath of fresh air aren't much different from someone who slaps his torturer, then goes back to counting how many more sticks will break over his behind.

I slipped out cautiously, fearful and on edge. Would I be seen by my uncle, who was forever lounging on his front stoop? If he did, he would interrupt one of his conversations with himself and, with a slow, dramatic turn of the head, say, "*Khayr*! Is everything all right? *Wayn ya m'sahhil?!*"

Then again, my other uncle, who had a view from his house on the whole town, might beat him to it.

If only the road that led to the main street and the world beyond didn't take me right past people's houses! As it was, though, leaving to go anywhere was like parading naked under the gaze of everybody who lived on the street—which meant, in effect, everybody in the village. After all, we only had one street, and all the houses were lined up along either side of it.

But I was going to Haifa. Haifa asked no questions and expected no answers. And neither did those who went there.

I managed to make it through the gauntlet, leaving the men behind to rearrange their questions and their boring days. As I walked down Haifa's main street, I undid another button in my suffocating blouse and let my hair blow in the wind with a red rose to caress it. Then I took off my shoes and walked down two long streets, observing people's calm faces and watching my reflection in shop display windows.

Walking into boutiques, I tried on things that would suit the dream of the future and put up with the discomfort of a new pair of earrings that my hair would keep hidden from my mother for a couple of weeks—or a couple of days.

I didn't prepare any argument to take back with me or try to come up with any reasons for my jaunt. Haifa itself was sufficient reason.

Three hours later I was on a bus headed back to my village. I was so engrossed in the trip, I nearly missed my stop. I took the details of the pleasant dream with me and covered my tracks with the skill of a seasoned thief.

Once again, I succeeded in slipping past the "man walls" before being stopped by an inquisitive glance from my uncle that nearly blew my cover.

Before the question came, I turned towards the street and walked along with confident steps.

But the question was more confident than I was.

"*Wayn ya m'sahhil?* And at this hour? Hurry on home now. Some girls have no shame."

Again, I turned in the direction of the house, my face smiling, but my back mocking the questions, and my waving hand mocking the silent answers.

Three Paintings

Fifteen

Three Paintings

⌒

It was velvety and black. This black, velvety dress resembled my life.

As I opened the wardrobe, its deep hue peeked out, sparking a memory that had faded with the passing of the days. How long was I going to hold onto it?

Until the image and the memory were complete? And what did I need with the memory? As for the image, it wasn't complicated. It wasn't lacking anything either.

I'd turned seventeen, and my cousin was three years older than me. I wasn't dying for love. But the waiting bothered me—the waiting for something to happen. Marriage would fill the emptiness of waiting, that was all. The image I had in mind was so simple, I could conjure it in a minute's time.

As for the three paintings, their details might take a couple of hours, but almost nobody asked about them.

I liked the dress for my henna party[12] even more than the wedding dress I'd borrowed from my cousin.

---

12 A bride's henna party takes place the day before the wedding in the bride's home and is a gathering of her close female friends and relatives. The celebration involves the application of henna to the bride's hands and feet in preparation for the wedding day.

It came pouring out of the wardrobe, and with it, a riot of fragrances that, having fermented over time, bombarded my nostrils with a thousand little stories. Had it been my choice? The henna dress was black, which I adore. I'd wanted it to be perfectly simple: long, velvety, and unadorned. And it was. But do women keep their wedding and henna dresses? If so, what for?

I knew its black hue would transcend the picture, the memory, and the details.

I used to carry it with me in a big bag whenever I visited Nazareth or Haifa. I had no idea what I was going to do with it. Once, I nearly threw it into the lap of a pretty young beggar. But before I could, she shot me a furious look and said, "The worst thing about begging is to come back with some dress whose time is past, or a bottle of stale perfume, or somebody's table scraps. It's all the same!"

I put it back in its bag before anybody saw me. Then I imagined her wearing a black henna party dress with her hand outstretched to passersby. I laughed at the thought. I remembered my own hand outstretched to the henna artist. She'd drawn a beautiful picture on it with crisscross, curved lines that cascaded down like a vine.

My three paintings would be beautiful too.

It wasn't waiting, or emptiness that would bring them into being, but coincidence. However, emptiness would be necessary in order for them to be completed: clean, velvety black fabric empty of any design.

"Does it meet the specifications?" the young artist asked me.

"Yes," I replied.

"Good. So bring it here and I'll draw you whatever you'd like."

I didn't have a clear idea of what I wanted. But whatever it was, it wasn't something that would break the blackness or fill the empty space.

"Do you like roses?"

"Yes. Who doesn't?"

"Do you like animals?"

"Yes. Who doesn't?"

"Okay, then, the fabric from the dress will be enough for three paintings: one of some stags grazing on grass, one of white roses, and another of red roses. Would you like that?"

"I'd like that a lot more than I like the wall the way it is now, and more than my corner next to the radio and the medicine bottle."

It still gives off a riot of fragrances that, having fermented over time, bombard my nostrils with a thousand little stories.

Only I don't smell them anymore. I just see them, and no one sees them but me.

The Day My Donkey Died

Sixteen

The Day My Donkey Died

⁓

Rarely does anybody ask her about her wedding date. But if they do, she says, "I got married the day my donkey died."

Her mother died; she doesn't remember when. Her father died two years later. She went on taking care of her little brother, who was two years younger than she was.

All her married brothers and sisters lived within shouting distance.

"Fedwa, fill the water jug from the spring!"

"Yes, ma'am."

"Fedwa, can't you see how my kids are wearing me out? You carry one of them."

"Yes, ma'am."

"Fedwa, you're so lazy! Who's going to go buy the salt and the flour?"

"Yes, ma'am."

"Fedwa…Fedwa…"

"Yes, ma'am…Yes, ma'am."

As annoying as it was to be bossed around by her married siblings, she figured serving them was more merciful than some potential marriage of her own. But she knew it was in the offing. Her older brother wouldn't let her wait till her eighteenth birthday, and he wouldn't ask for her opinion either.

Meanwhile, the good-natured she-ass was her faithful companion wherever she went.

She couldn't count the number of times she'd slept on the ground, shaded for hours by her long-suffering donkey. She would sing her songs she'd memorized from weddings and funerals and tell her little stories, some about things that had happened, and some about things that hadn't. She rarely rode her, and if she did so, out of necessity, she would give her a heartfelt and tender apology.

One day Fedwa's sister-in-law saw her from a distance carrying a water jug on her head, steadying the jug with one hand and with the other, patting her donkey on the back as the two strolled side by side.

"All the women are gossiping about that sister of yours!" she whispered to her husband.

In the Jewish settlement where she bought all her family's food and supplies, she was known as "the girl with the donkey," the one who talked to her donkey more than she talked to them.

When she went out to get things, she'd be gone till evening. Sometimes she'd stay the night at her uncle's house and forget the yeast and dried milk on her donkey's back.

"What's the story with that animal? And where do you go with her?"

She knew her brothers were bothered by her ways. Some of them might even have thought she was possessed by jinn or touched in the head. After all, who sings to a riding animal? And who would marry a girl who sings to a donkey, even if she's pretty and has a warm voice?

A suitor had come from a distant village, and she didn't give much thought to his homeliness, or even to his rudeness and stupidity. What really bothered her was the fact that he walked, talked, and even sat like some lifeless idol, and that he made fun of her and her donkey.

"*Widditch tatalli`iha bi jihazitch*? You gonna take it with you as part of your trousseau?" he joked crudely.

Her brother shot her an angry wink. "Don't you dare answer that," he hissed under his breath. "Thanks to you, we've become a laughing stock!"

The wedding date was coming up, and every day she said goodbye to another stone along her path. She was making room for the boulders that would come and occupy her spirit. She was memorizing the features of the brief, simple life she was leaving behind. It had been free of any complications to speak of apart from her silent friend, to whom she grew steadily more attached as her brother grew steadily more furious.

"Tomorrow they're going to escort you to your husband, and you'll become a sensible woman who only talks to people. You understand?"

She nodded without a word.

What her brother didn't know was that she would talk to nothing but the walls until her senseless husband bit the dust.

The grief she felt over the death of her donkey on her wedding day overshadowed her even greater grief over a life that had slipped through her fingers.

Whenever her husband mocked her and made jokes about her relationship with riding animals, she would retort, "I married you the day my donkey died."

Then she would whisper to herself, "... although she didn't just die. She was murdered."

God Bless Town Field!

Seventeen

"God Bless Toun Field!"

⌐⌐

Toun Field, the only flat spot in the mountain village, was a dusty lot open from the north and south. From the west it was bounded by half a mountain that had escaped the devastation of stone quarries and the Nakba that had been suffered by the terrain and people alike, and to its east lay three abandoned wells with large mouths. They weren't very deep, but they posed a threat to grownups and children alike, whether they were running after the ball, or chasing the remains of daylight between mid-afternoon and sundown.

Aunt Aisha—paternal aunt to half the family's young men and women, and maternal aunt to the other half—would shake the water off her hands, dry them on the hem of her dress, and then go running after the players, warning them not to get too close to the wells, or reminding them that it was about to get dark. She kept one eye on the ground, and the other on the sky. When people criticized her for running around the field the way she did, she'd say, "Well, they're so excited, they're not going to see two inches in front of them. So how are they going to see the goal sandwiched between two rocks?"

The men attributed her presence among them to her good-hearted concern for them. As for the women, they attributed it to a pathological nosiness that had grown as she got older, and which made no exception for the men's space.

One afternoon her questions came raining down on the kids cheering on their friends and waiting for their turn to play:

"What the hell—why did you kick Omar out of the game?"

"Why didn't you count Hussein's goal?"

"What does 'foul' mean?"

None of them bothered to answer. Their eyes and ears were fixed on the ball.

Aunt Aisha had learned the rules of football and the field to spite her illiteracy, and to spite all the males of the extended family who had mastered the art of football and of reading to boot. When she was a little girl, she'd watched them enviously as they headed out for the school in a distant village, and later on as they started writing letters to sweethearts.

But now here she was, registering a victory over them as she shouted at a lazy player, "Hurry up, you. Run, run, you dumb-bell! The goal's free!"

Her sorrow over Toun Field exceeded even her sorrow over the wooden hut that had been demolished by bulldozers. In her sturdy new house, she missed the pleasure of running around the field. She missed the dust stirred up by feet running after a ball, and the smell of perspiration as the young men of the family scattered to their huts when darkness fell. The "genius" television screen had deprived her of all that, leaving her nothing but the sound of her voice mingled with the voices of the old players. Their potbellies had turned them into couch potatoes sprawled on sponge mattresses, only to jump up suddenly if a friend made a goal, or kick a pack of cigarettes if an enemy scored.

"Damn, I miss the old days, the days of Toun Field!" she would sigh before yelling at the player on the TV screen, "Run, Zidane, run! The goal's free!"

As usual before every match, she prepared a big pot of tea, cold juices, sandwiches and nuts—everything that would ensure that she wouldn't have to get up from her place to meet the demands of her importunate husband. Then, after drying her hands on the edge of her thobe, she sat down cross-legged on the reed mat in front of the big screen and waited for the match between France and Italy to begin. For the first time since the village was demolished and she took refuge in another village, she could smell the dust of a football field, as the aroma of the green stadium wafted out of the giant screen.

She was always worried about Zidane displaying his vulnerabilities. During any moments of weakness or inattention, all her senses went on high alert as she called out to him, using his full Arabic name, determined not to let some foreign letters break her remaining teeth.

Then suddenly her husband began to choke and gestured for her to bring him the asthma inhaler.

"I swear to God, I'm not getting up," she retorted.

He cursed her, struggling to catch his breath, and threw a cushion her way. Grudgingly, she got up and hurried back to him with the inhaler. At that moment, between the living room and the kitchen shelves, cries of disappointment shook the walls of the house. "The well!" she said, her heart sinking.

Back in the living room, the looks on people's faces told her nothing. However, through a slow-motion replay, the screen told her what had happened during her moment's absence. Zidane had approached an Italian player, butted him in the chest and knocked him to the ground! The shot was replayed once, twice, ten times, and with every replay she looked daggers at her husband. When his breathing had finally gone back to normal, she said, "Next time you're going to die after the match is over!"

Many years have passed since that moment when she was forced to leave her spot, betrayed by both her intuition and Zidane's head. She aged and her eyesight deteriorated. Her husband aged, and his heart got weaker. But as the family expanded into a tribe of children, grandchildren and great-grand-children, her passion remained a loyal guard, not budging from in front of the screen until the match was over. As for her husband, he would keep his eyes on the screen, postponing his insults until the referee's whistle sounded and—whether beaming with contentment or snarling in frustration—his wife rose from her place.

Queens of
Darkness

Eighteen

Queens of Darkness

ᶜᵒ

The queens of darkness don't know that this is who they are. Sovereignty is a quarry they've never been trained to hunt. Nor does it occupy their thoughts. Rather, the only quarry they know is life itself—life unadorned.

At the age of thirty, every one of them adopts a ready-made, prepackaged reply to every stupid or existential question. The question might be, for example, "How are you?" "What would happiness look like to you?" "When will you depart?"

She pulls an answer out of the sleeve of her wandering. "How would I know?" she says. "Life will end when it ends."

It's a reply that resembles God's true promises. It isn't a supplication. It isn't an entreaty. Rather, it's an accurate, un adorned description of a universal condition. There's no use arguing with it, rejecting it, or rebelling against it. This life will pass away, and all it requires of her is to surrender. At the same time, there is no harm in giving it a little push towards the last bend in the road.

As she enters her glorious forties, the countdown, or the calculation of lost time (as some women think of it) begins in a small back room amid giant kettles that have been passed down generation after generation along with kohl sticks and a certain understanding of happiness. Here it's important to know which direction to stir the cooked milk, when to add the seasonings, where secrets are kept, and how old stories are divided up.

Here, life's details are enveloped in silence, while gestures are the luxury of those who are in a hurry. As for the spatial void, it is occupied by giant kettles, bags of vegetables, and poorly calculated, sweeping disappointments. The conversations about men in the darkness—on the edge of bitterness and hatred, the edge of fear, the edge of pleasure—are never closed, and never slip.

"The widow isn't black," says the darkness.

"Men (all of them) are the protectors and maintainers of women (all of them)," say the walls of darkness.

Then suddenly the light comes pouring in, and the glare in the corner calls out like sin. Each of them murmurs to her broken shadow, "I really don't know…"

"Light follows upon knowledge, and philosophy is the daughter of darkness." But nobody says this.

Mercifully for them, the queens of darkness don't know.

Acknowledgements

I thank the women who believed in my stories, our stories, the stories of the women of the village of Dhail El E'rj. I thank in particular Reem Ghanayem, Nancy Roberts, Sofia Rehman and Archna Sharma for the work and love each one poured into this book. For believing in the stories and voices of Palestinian women and girls.

Sheikha Helawy
Sheikha was born in Dhail El E'rj, an unrecognized Bedouin village near Haifa. She now lives in Jaffa and is working on her PhD on "New Diaspora in Arab Women's Writing". She is a lecturer in Arab Feminism at Ben-Gurion University. Sheikha has published several novels and short story collections, with many of her works having been translated into English, German, French and Bulgarian. This is the first time a complete work of hers is being made available in English.

Nancy Roberts
Nancy Roberts is a freelance Arabic-to-English translator and editor who spent twenty-five years in the Middle East (Lebanon, Kuwait and Jordan). Her translation of Ghada Samman's *Beirut '75* won the 1994 Arkansas Arabic Translation Award, and she was awarded the 2018 Sheikh Hamad Prize for Translation and International Understanding for her translation of Ibrahim Nasrallah's *Gaza Weddings* and other works in Nasrallah's corpus. In addition to literature, she enjoys translating materials on political, economic and environmental issues, human rights, international development, Islamic thought and movements, and interreligious dialogue. She is based in the Chicago suburbs.

113

Anna Morrison

Anna is an award-winning book cover designer, art director, and illustrator. She has spent many years working in-house for various publishers including Penguin Random House, 4th Estate, and Pushkin Press. She now works as a freelancer. You can find more of Anna's beautiful designs at: www.annamorrison.com.